Debbie's dream

GILBERT DELAHAYE - MARCEL MARLIER

award publications

It was a freezing cold day. Snow was thick on the ground, and an icy wind was blowing. Debbie was so pleased to see the snow that she rushed out after breakfast to play with her friends in the park.

But she had forgotten to put on her coat and gloves and hat. When she got home she was shivering with cold, and her teeth wouldn't stop chattering. Her mother took one look at her and said, "Let's get you straight into a warm bath. That should get the chill out of your bones!"

But Debbie still shivered.

The next morning she woke up with a streaming cold. Her nose was running, her eyes were red and sore, and her head and throat ached. Outside she could hear her friends calling to her to come and play. "We're going tobogganing," they cried. "Why don't you come with us?"
But Debbie's head was spinning and her legs felt like cotton wool.

"You'd better stay in bed," her mother said. "Have a good sleep and later on I'll ask the doctor to take a look at you." Debbie was very glad to lie back on the pillow and close her eyes. She was very sleepy. . .

Soon she was having a lovely dream. A gentle snowman was dancing with her, and he was singing, "Come away to the mountains, Debbie. Come to the land of the winter king. I will show you palaces of ice and trees of silver. And you will eat the sparkling snowfruit hanging from their branches."

It was an enchanting place, despite the snow and ice. It seemed as warm as a summer's day, and the air was filled with the scent of a thousand flowers. There was sweet music everywhere.

Then the dream faded, and Debbie began to wake up. "I was so happy there," she thought.

The doctor came. He took her temperature, listened to her chest, and made her open her mouth and say "aah". "Well, you've got a nasty sore throat," he said. "But another day in bed and plenty to drink, and you'll soon be better."

All the time Debbie was sipping her drink she was thinking about her dream. "How I wish I could go there and see the winter king's palace of ice," she sighed.

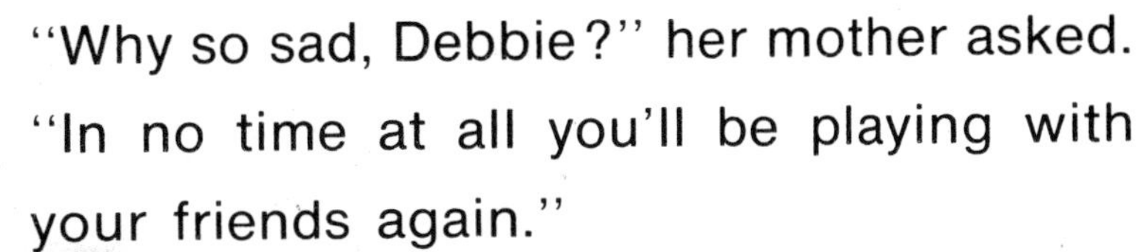

"Why so sad, Debbie?" her mother asked. "In no time at all you'll be playing with your friends again."

Debbie told her all about the dream, about the trees of silver and the snowfruit and how she longed to see and taste them. "Oh Debbie," said her mother, "I can see I'll have to send Grandpa to talk to you."

Soon Debbie heard a familiar voice at the door. "What's all this? Debbie in bed and unhappy–we'll have to do something about that."

Ever since she could remember Debbie had loved to talk to her grandfather.

He could always make her laugh when she was sad and he told the funniest stories in the world.

Now she started to tell him about her dream. She said she felt sad because the land of the winter king had been so beautiful and she didn't know how she could go there again.

"Well, you know," said Grandpa, "dreams sometimes come true–though not always in the way we expect."

Debbie felt a lot happier right away. She knew that her grandfather always told her the truth.
Her Mother said she was well enough for her friends to come and see her, and soon they were all telling her the latest news.

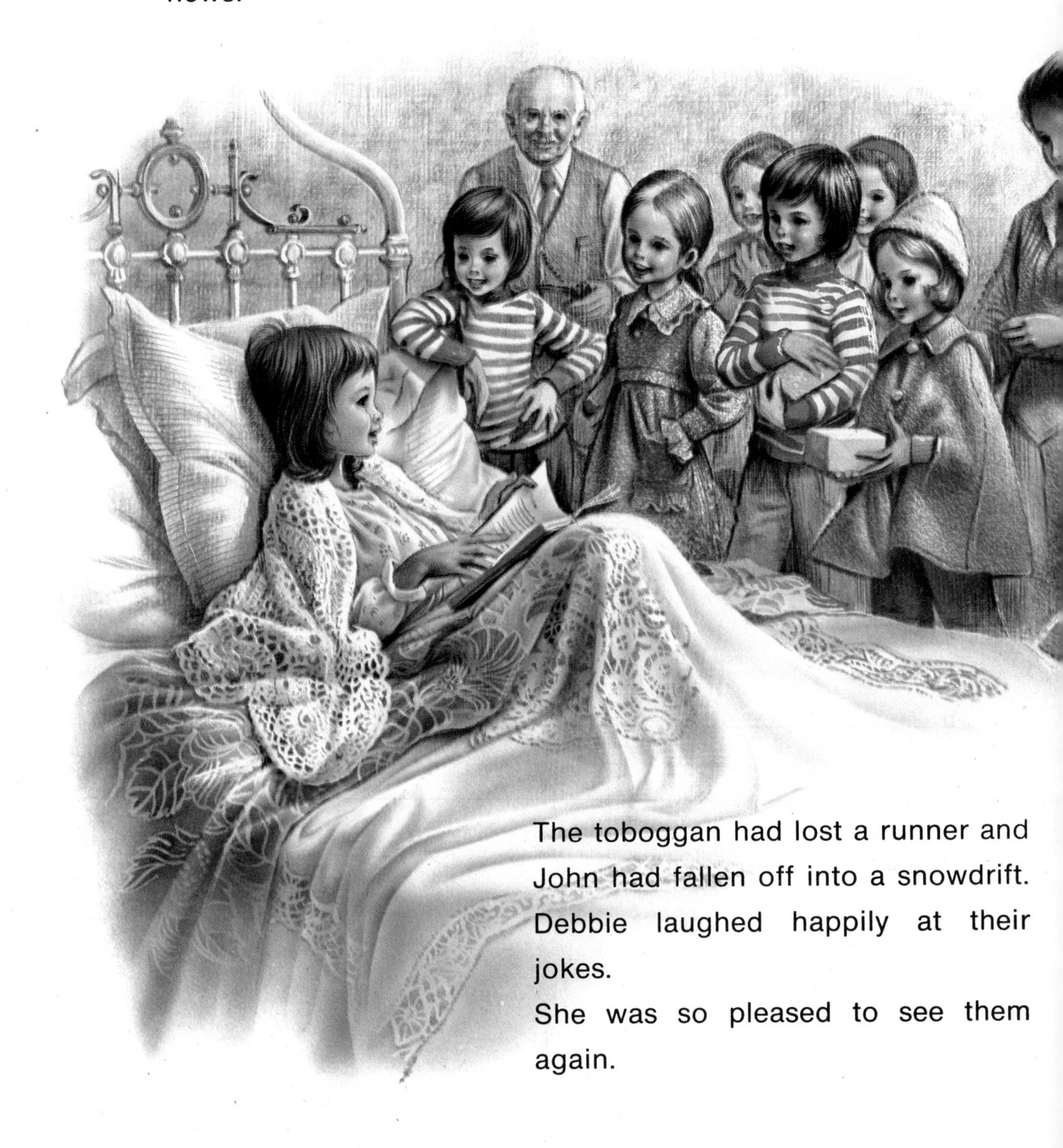

The toboggan had lost a runner and John had fallen off into a snowdrift. Debbie laughed happily at their jokes.
She was so pleased to see them again.

The next morning Debbie was thrilled to get a letter from Aunt Betty. It said that Grandpa had told her about Debbie's dream.

"Do you know there are trees of silver in my garden? They may not be the same as the winter king's but they are very pretty. As soon as spring is here why don't you come and see for yourself?"

That afternoon Debbie watched television with her father. It was her favorite cartoon film, but she couldn't keep her mind on it.

She was too busy thinking about Aunt Betty's letter. "Trees of silver in my garden"–what could she mean? Aunt Betty lived in the country, but Debbie had seen nothing like that when she had last been there at the end of the summer. The trees had been green and covered with apples.

Debbie longed for the spring to come. She couldn't wait to discover what Aunt Betty had meant.

At last the snow began to melt, and little by little the weather turned warmer. Then one day as Debbie sat at the window she heard the birds singing again in the garden. A robin landed on a branch next to her and Debbie saw that the trees were bursting into leaf.

The crocuses and daffodils were pushing their bright heads through the grass. Without her noticing it, spring had arrived at last.

Debbie ran to find paper and pen so that she could write to Aunt Betty.

"Dear Aunt Betty,

The sun is shining every day now, and the flowers are out in the garden. Spring is really here. Can I come and see your trees of silver? Is it really true? I have thought about them every day. I will arrive on Saturday if I may. With love from Debbie."

Debbie was so excited as she began to get ready for her visit. She loved going on journeys. There was always so much to see, and it was such fun choosing what clothes to take with her. By this time tomorrow she would see Aunt Betty's trees for herself. . .

As soon as they reached her Aunt's house Debbie rushed into the garden. The apple trees. . . they were covered in tiny white blossom!

So that was it! Sparkling in the sun, they did look as if they were all of silver. Debbie ran backwards and forwards through the trees, smelling the blossom, listening to the birds. The silvery flowers were everywhere.

It was so like her dream–but so different! She ran happily up to Aunt Betty. "It's not like the land of the winter king," she laughed. "But it's all so pretty.
Thank you for showing me your trees of silver. They're even lovelier than I expected."
"I'm glad you like them," replied Aunt Betty, giving her a hug.
"You've waited so patiently to see them!"